MOONDOG

By Alice Hoffman and Wolfe Martin

Illustrated by Yumi Heo

SCHOLASTIC PRESS · NEW YORK

Text copyright © 2004 by Alice Hoffman and Wolfe Martin • Illustrations copyright © 2004 by Yumi Heo

All rights reserved. Published by Scholastic Press, a division of Scholastic Inc., *Publishers since 1920*. SCHOLASTIC,

SCHOLASTIC PRESS, and associated logos are trademarks and/or registered trademarks of Scholastic Inc.

Library of Congress Cataloging-in-Publication Data

Hoffman, Alice.

Moondog / by Alice Hoffman and Wolfe Martin; illustrated by Yumi Heo.— 1st ed.   p. cm.

Summary: When a family adopts a well-behaved puppy that they name Angel, everything is fine until the next full moon.

ISBN 0-439-09861-0

[1. Dogs—Fiction. 2. Animals—Infancy—Fiction. 3. Werewolves—Fiction. 4. Halloween—Fiction.] I. Martin, Wolfe.

II. Heo, Yumi, ill. III. Title.

PZ7.H67445 Mo 2004   [Fic]—dc22   2003019664

10 9 8 7 6 5 4 3 2 1   04 05 06 07 08

Printed in Singapore   46

First edition, August 2004

The text type was set in 16-point Geometric 231 Bold

The display type was set in Beesknees

The illustrations were done in oil, acrylic, and collage.

Book design by Kristina Albertson

TO OUR OWN MOONDOG, ANGEL
—W.M. and A.H.

FOR OWEN and MOLLY, WOOF! WOOF!
—Y.H.

ONE NIGHT, WHEN

the moon was full, in a town not far from here, where every day was sunny and every night was clear, a shadowy figure crept into the McKenzie's yard. Whomever or whatever it was didn't stay long, only long enough to place a basket on the porch steps before slinking away.

Michael McKenzie and his sister, Hazel, thought they heard growling and howling in their dreams. In the morning, they peeked out the window, and sure enough, someone had been there. Their yard was destroyed! The flower garden had been trampled, the porch steps chewed into splinters, the crab apples and maples looked more like toothpicks than trees! But something had escaped whatever terrible thing had been in their garden: There at the front door was a basket. Inside was the sweetest, most darling puppy anyone had ever seen.

Michael and Hazel begged their mother and pleaded with their father and at last the puppy was theirs. They named him Angel, because that's what he seemed to be. No puppy had ever been easier to train. After only a few weeks, Angel sat on command and rolled over and wagged his tail and never made little puddles where little puddles shouldn't be. He fetched and came when called; he climbed into their laps and licked their faces. Other puppies might chew and snap, they might chomp on shoes and toys, but not Angel.

Even Michael and Hazel's parents, who had
never wanted a dog in the first place, had to admit they
were lucky to have a pup like Angel. But in the last week
of the month, on a dark night when clouds covered
the full, orange moon, there was a terrible storm.
Michael and Hazel woke in the middle of the night to clattering
and thumping, crashing and smashing. They rushed downstairs,
two steps at a time, but they arrived too late!

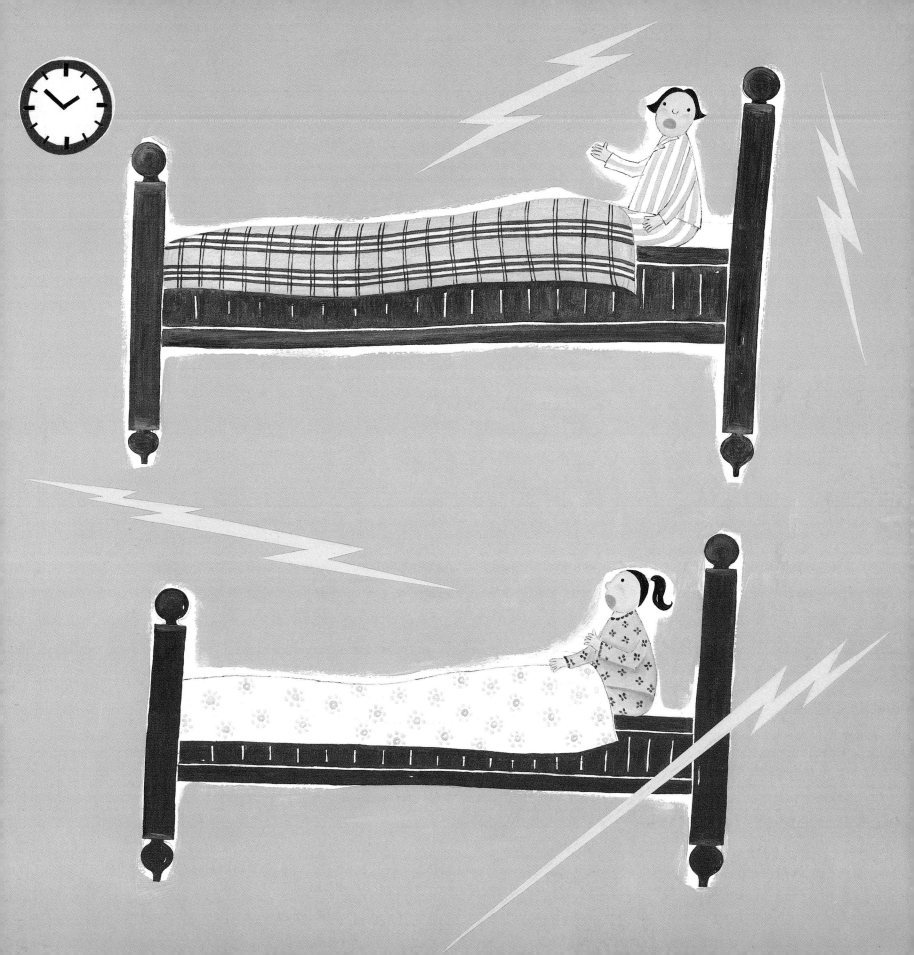

The kitchen was already destroyed, but that wasn't the worst of it. Angel was gone! He wasn't under the pile of wood that had once been the table and chairs. He wasn't hiding in the cabinets or cowering under the stove avoiding whatever terrible creature had been there. Who could have done this? The kitchen door was wide open, hanging on one hinge, swaying back and forth in the wind. A bag of flour had been spilled all over the floor, and something had walked through the mess. There were huge powdery footsteps, as big as a wolf's, headed out the door.

Hazel and Michael followed the white footsteps along the street, through backyards. The clouds were gone, and the orange moon lit up the sky. The wind shook the bare, black trees and made them whimper and wail. At last, they came to Miss Eleanor Mingle's house, with its old, twisted vines and rambling black roses. On the stone path that was covered with moss, something metallic shone: Angel's silver name tag.

No one had ever been brave enough to walk up Miss Mingle's path. The grown-ups in town said don't be silly, but many were scared themselves. Why, the policemen were too frightened to sell Miss Mingle raffle tickets, and even the Girl Scouts wouldn't bring cookies to her door. No gardener would work in her yard. The boy who delivered her groceries only came at high noon, when the sun was at its brightest, and he ran like a skunk through her moldy garden where it was said she grew horseradish, stinkweed, and a beautiful red flower that smelled like old shoes.

But Michael and Hazel had no choice but to
go forward and rescue their pup. Under the
light of the orange moon, they carefully edged
down the path to Miss Mingle's. They told
each other they weren't afraid, but when they
heard barking, they froze. The only thing scarier
than Miss Mingle was her nasty dog, Bunny.
Everyone in town was scared of Bunny, who was
big and shaggy and had especially large teeth.

"Maybe Bunny is the one who's been wrecking our house," Hazel whispered. "I'll bet she is."

"Don't be dumb," Michael said. "Bunny is always tied up." Or at least he hoped so. They crept to the door and knocked, but no one answered. So around the house they went, determined to find their puppy. When they reached the back porch, they wiped the soot and dust from the kitchen window. Once they saw inside, they burst right through the back door. There in the kitchen was Miss Mingle feeding Angel a bowl of white foaming stew made from stinkweed and horseradish and that strange red flower that only grew in her garden.

"Stop that!" the children hollered. "That's our puppy!" they cried.

"Oh my stars," Miss Eleanor Mingle said when she saw them. She nearly dropped her horrible brew when Angel yipped with joy and jumped to greet the children.

Bunny, who they always feared, ducked under the table and covered her eyes with her paws. "What are you doing to our puppy?" Hazel demanded to know.

"If you must know, he's Bunny's puppy," Miss Mingle informed them. "Although Bunny and I agreed that you children would be the perfect ones to raise him. Not everyone can deal with a moondog, you see. Or a werepup, if you prefer. It's a big responsibility, especially until you train them. And it used to be much worse before I figured out the ingredients of this brew," Miss Mingle said, offering the children her special half-moon cookies. "I've had this kind of dog since I was little, but I'm getting too old to care for another. When Bunny had a pup, I had to give him away. The mixture I was feeding him stops moondogs from becoming werepups on the nights of the full moon. I just wish I'd known this remedy when I was your age. I never could have friends come to visit for fear the moon would appear and my dogs would change. I let the vines grow higher and I planted anything with thorns, just to keep people away and protect my moondogs. But now I'm all alone."

Miss Eleanor Mingle
was actually crying. Hazel
felt so bad, she offered her very
own handkerchief, the one with the
yellow ducks that her Aunt Josie had
sent her on her birthday. Miss Eleanor
Mingle had given them Angel, now it was up to
them to give something back. Michael crunched a
half-moon cookie, which was the most delicious treat he'd
ever had, and patted good old Bunny, who wasn't scary in the
least. Then and there he came up with a plan to help Miss Mingle.

The next full moon was on Halloween night, the perfect time for a party. They spent the day mowing the lawn for Miss Mingle and tying back the black roses; they sprayed

the stinkweed with cologne and gave Angel and Bunny a buttermilk bath. All that day, Miss Mingle baked, and by evening the whole town smelled like cookies.

Trick-or-treaters who had always avoided Miss Mingle's house found themselves walking up the mossy path, and many brought their parents along. The house looked so bright and friendly, the black roses smelled like chocolate cake, and people in town wondered why they hadn't thought to visit Miss Mingle before. Everyone loved her special half-moon cookies, and they particularly enjoyed the dogs, who were dressed up like werewolves that sat beside the front door.

Michael and Hazel and Miss Mingle all agreed on this:

Every puppy deserves to be a

at least one night a year!